The Adventures of Timmy the Turtle

Timmy at the Pond

Frank Goddard

AuthorHouse
1663 Liberty Drive
Bloomington, IN 47403
www.authorhouse.com
Phone: 1-800-839-8640

Published by AuthorHouse 04/12/2013

ISBN: 978-1-4817-3545-2 (sc)
978-1-4817-3546-9 (e)

Library of Congress Control Number: 2013906004

authorHOUSE®

Once upon a time, there was a little turtle named Timmy. Timmy got his name from two bright little sisters that decided they wanted a pet turtle.

Timmy lived in a little fish tank that had four glass walls, and he swam and swam but could not get past that unknown force that prevented him from leaving. Timmy wondered what was holding him in and keeping him from going where he wanted to go.

Then one day, Timmy grew bigger and stronger and started to worry all the other animals in the tank.

8

Timmy was taken by their father to another place where he had more room. It was a small pond with rocks, a waterfall, goldfish, and green leaves all around. It was a happy place and perfect for Timmy to grow in, but Timmy was still curious ever since his experience with that unknown force of those glass walls.

Timmy stayed in the pond for many days, until one day Timmy decided to go out on his own. *"Boy, was it a big world out there!"* And Timmy was excited to see and experience all the little things that made up a turtle's life.

Timmy set out on his journey up over the rock and out of the pond, through the heavy, green plant life. "Boy, was the green plant large!" Timmy thought. "Man, I hope I make my way back," but Timmy kept going and pressing on.

Timmy walked over all kinds of terrain and into a very large fence. "Oh, no!" Timmy thought. "I'm trapped again, just like I was in the tank." But not for long! Timmy kept looking with his little eyes, and finally he found a spot where he could squeeze his little body through the fence and away he went! But now Timmy was farther from his home at the old pond, with no certainty that he would ever make it back. But Timmy kept going.

Days went by, and Timmy ran into all kinds of animals. Birds were catching bugs, and wasps were collecting mud for their nest. Timmy kept on going. He found lots of new tasty foods, including grasshoppers, ants, crickets, beetles, and worms. Then suddenly Timmy stopped and thought, *"Where's the pond with all the water, green leaves, and my fish friends, Freddie, Fran, Fergie, and Faith? Oh no! What have I done?"*

16

The next day, Timmy heard a noise, a loud chopping and buzzing. He hurried away from it, but it kept getting closer and closer and louder and louder. *"Oh no! It's a lawn mower coming right at me!"* he exclaimed. He ran fast but could not outrun the giant man pushing the mower. Timmy ducks his head and prays.

Suddenly, the loud noise stopped getting closer, and Timmy was relieved. The man had seen Timmy just about the time Timmy was wishing he was back at the old pond.

The man was coming toward Timmy, so he closed his eyes and prayed. To Timmy's surprise, the giant man picked Timmy up and carried him away. Timmy was scared to death and feared heights, still praying as he was looking down from way up.

Then suddenly, Timmy was back at the old rock pond. He was safe again, telling his story to all his friends, Freddie, Fran, Fergie, and Faith, about how he was saved when he prayed.

THE END

CPSIA information can be obtained
at www.ICGtesting.com
Printed in the USA
LVIW020711010513
331645LV00002B

9 781481 735452